BY DR. ALEX KODIATH

Order this book online at www.trafford.com
or email orders@trafford.com

Most Trafford titles are also available at major online book retailers.

Print information available on the last page.

ISBN: 978-1-4907-5693-6 (sc)
       978-1-4907-5692-9 (e)

Our mission is to efficiently provide the world's finest, most comprehensive book publishing
service, enabling every author to experience success. To find out how to publish your book,
your way, and have it available worldwide, visit us online at www.trafford.com

Trafford rev. 08/28/2015

 www.trafford.com

North America & international
toll-free: 1 888 232 4444 (USA & Canada)
fax: 812 355 4082

Table of Contents

Acknowledgements

This is another elephant story. In writing this book, I continue to incorporate leadership concepts, life values, travel issues, and spiritual principles. It is up to the readers to recognize these concepts. Social media is saturated with violence and negative stories. Children need positive stories to strengthen their leadership skills. If through these stories I am able to nurture and facilitate some constructive and transforming values, then I will have achieved my vision in writing this story.

My wife Mary always gives unconditional support as well as constructive guidance in developing the story into a book. She has read and re-read this book. My daughter Pria helped, helping me to see this book through children's eyes.

I also want to thank Ann Aubrey Hanson and Dileep Kumar for shaping the book as a readable, artistic, and colorful work. In anticipation, I thank all the future readers who will take time to tell me about the good and the weak parts of the book. I will cherish those comments in my future endeavors.
Thanks,

Dr. K
akodiath@gmail.com

Dedication

Dedicated to the humanitarian couple

Maxien and Gary Kreitzer

for their unconditional support for the education of children.

The Author is grateful to the following persons:

Mary Kodiath, Ann Aubrey Hanson
Gops and Dileep of Design Hub

INTRODUCTION

Kris: The Elephant at Sea,

this is a second adventure of Kris the Elephant. The first adventure is illustrated in the book: Elephant Escapes to an Island. This adventure at sea starts with a journey with students who were travelling abroad in a ship. The ship was heading toward the United States, though there were several planned stops, such as at Denis Island. Kris was transported to this island to lead a centenary celebration while the students had an educational visit to learn about culture and tradition of the Island.

During this trip, Kris and his caretakers Jojo and George are able to attend some English language lessons with some international students. The book also depicts some of the cultural celebrations of the southern India. While everybody enjoys the students' demonstrations of their understanding of the culture and traditions in dramatic play, the Somali pirates take control of the ship and take hostage of all American students and teachers.

In this chaotic situation, Kris runs wild and falls into the sea. What happens to the students, teachers, and crew? This is the story of how an elephant who fell into the sea became instrumental in saving everyone in the ship. Read the fascinating adventure of Kris, the Elephant.

Dr. K

Chapter 1

Kris, Jojo, and George get ready for the
journey to Saint-Denis Island

Kris at the Center of Centennial Celebration

I am Kris the elephant. It is my pet name. I really like it when people call me Kris, though my full name is Krishna. In my first adventure, I helped save Crow Island and its people. Now I am called to adventures at sea beyond anyone's imagination!

It all started when a rich man from Saint-Denis Island bought me from Sampath, my owner in India. The rich man wanted to celebrate his company's 100-year ownership of the private island. He had invited all the celebrities who had been married on the island, and he needed an elephant to lead the ceremonial procession. There was only one elephant in the world that he knew had the special curve on its back where the city emblem could sit during the long procession. I was that elephant!

My owner told the Indian government that I would be rented to Saint-Denis Island for the ceremony, but the greedy Sampath sold me! One of the conditions of the sale was that my mahouts, the trainers Jojo and George, accompany me on the journey.

Chapter 2

Kris's Dream

**Jojo, George, and I were excited
about taking a trip on a cruise ship.
I began to dream about the journey where
I am travelling on a ship, and it is quite
a different trip from a truck ride. I will
travel across the Arabian Sea and then across
the Indian Ocean. I am also thrilled that I
will be the main attraction in the centenary
ceremony, carrying the city's Golden Emblem
on my back. This is special. I am special. I
can't wait!**

Kris and the Passports

Both Jojo and George were so excited about
the trip to a new land on a cruise ship.
They got their pictures taken for the passports
and visas. I was happy the passport office
placed my picture on my travel documents,
too. Jojo asked George the questions I also
heard about passports and visas. What are
these things and why do we need them? Before
becoming a mahout, George had worked
for a travel company, so he knew that when
someone leaves their country to visit another
country, the passport is necessary as a travel
document.

Chapter 3

Passport photos of Jojo, Kris, and George

The passport tells people in one country what country you are from. He explained that the visa is another travel document, and it gives a person permission to visit another country. Hearing this, I wondered, "Do birds need travel documents?"

Chapter 4

Kris on a crane being transported to a ship in Kochi Harbor

Kochi Harbor

The beautiful cruise ship had docked in Kochi Port. Kochi is an international city in Kerala, which is in southern India. People were all gathered around the dock to catch a glimpse of an elephant being loaded on to a cruise ship. I was in a cage strapped to a solid wood platform. A crane slowly lifted me high into the sky. I was a bit concerned being so high, but when I looked around the site, my fear vanished and I began to enjoy the natural beauty of Kochi Harbor.

I will never forget the sight of rows of fishing nets moving up and down against the backdrop of the spectacular golden sun setting to the west. As the crane swung me toward the ship, I noticed the beauty of buildings on the shore, both small and towering. There were several huge ships from different nations anchored around the harbor, with their national flags flying in the evening breeze. It looked like a marvelous parade was coming down the docks.

When I was lowered on to the ship deck, Jojo and George were ready to guide me to a secured area. As I reached the lower deck, I heard thunderous applause from the upper deck.

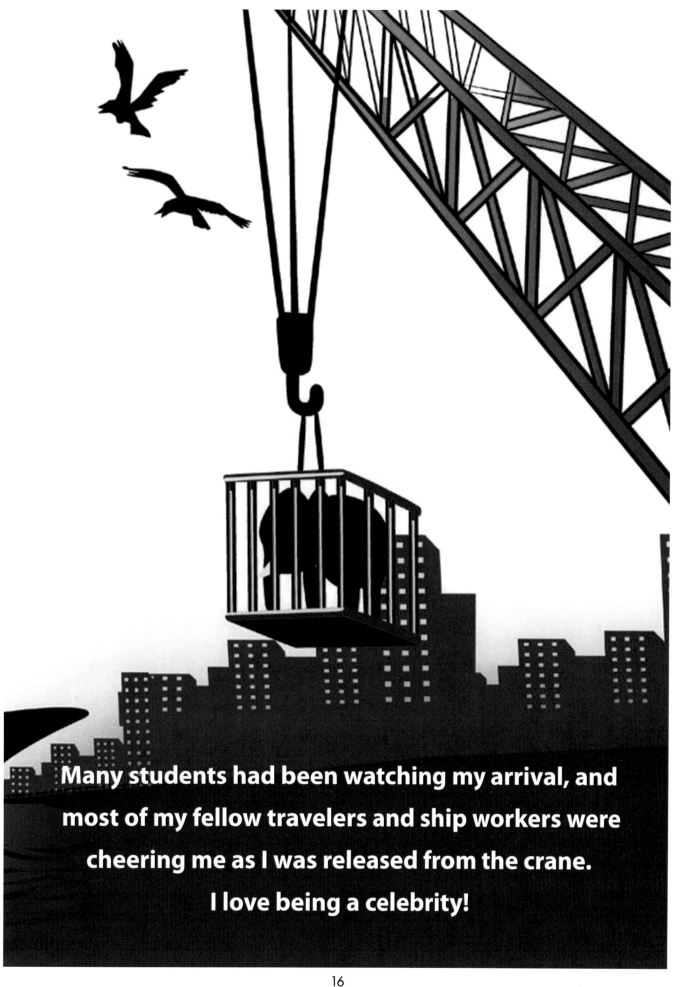

Many students had been watching my arrival, and most of my fellow travelers and ship workers were cheering me as I was released from the crane.
I love being a celebrity!

Kris On Board

Jojo and George placed me in my very own holding cell and secured me by a chain on my leg. With a loud whistle, the ship began her journey to the United States of America, stopping on the way in several countries, and at Saint-Denis Island. This island is off the east coast of Africa in the Indian Ocean. As the ship began to move, I was disappointed not to be able to see what was going on outside. There were no windows in my cell. When we hit open water, I began to feel seasick. If elephants could turn green, I'm sure I did. Jojo and George tried to calm me down, but in vain. My stomach was turning somersaults and I started shuffling in place and swinging my head. Oh, I was going to be sick!

Chapter 5

Kris and his trainers walk around the ship

They brought a student veterinarian who knew how
to treat large animals like me.
Her name was Grace and she was young
and beautiful. She appeared to have no fear
about examining me. First, she tried to give me a
banana. I took a small bite but couldn't even eat my
favorite food. Then she allowed me to smell and feel
her hand so I could get to know her.
Once I was calm, she examined me and came up with
a treatment plan. She gave me some nice treats with
pills hidden in them to prevent my seasickness. I
could taste the pills but the treats were nice,
so I ate them.
The medicine worked for a while then I started
feeling sick again, and started thrashing
and shaking my head.

But Dr. Grace was sharp.
She knew the real needs of a large animal like me.
She asked Jojo and George to take me for walks
around the ship. Funny enough, the patient's
wish and doctor's order were the same! I was
so relieved. I am an outdoor guy. Fresh air was
a tonic for me. I liked the student doctor; she
was graceful. She was my Grace.

Chapter 6

Kris attends class,
sitting on a wooden stool

Study at Sea: Students from the USA

Our ship was carrying students back to the United States after their Study at Sea program, during which time students from various universities visit several foreign nations. This group had just visited Kochi in India.

The students and their teachers got to know me well during my daily walks with Jojo and George. I was even welcomed by the instructors to observe their classes.

I even had my own four-legged stool to sit on in the classroom. Only thing is that I had to be careful not to sit on my tail!

The classes were in English, and Jojo and George and I only know Malayalam, the native language of Kerala State in India, so I didn't understand much, but I enjoyed just being with the students and they enjoyed talking to me.

By good fortune, there were some Chinese, German, and Mexican students in the group, and they had special English language classes, which Jojo, George, and I were delighted to attend. We could practice our new English vocabulary with the American students.

Our friendship grew day by day. My new friends brought me their fruit from breakfast, lunch, and dinner. I quickly learned the names of those fruits in English. Apple became my favorite fruit, after banana, of course. We did not get bananas every day, but when the students learned that I liked bananas, they saved them for me. That was nice.

Chapter 7

Kris walks on the ship,
greeting his friends

Kris Keeps Fit

Even though I had ankle restraints,
Jojo and George took me for a walk every evening.
I looked forward to these daily walks when I could
see the students and other people. Everyone on
board began to see me as a pet and began to interact
with me freely. Jojo and George always held onto my
lead but I felt like I was free. Fresh air and
sunshine made me very happy.
Jojo and George were good to me on the trip, giving
me fresh food, clean water, and lots of exercise. My
daily walk also kept me physically fit.
I was a happy sailor.
Until one night,
when something terrible happened.

Chapter 8

Kris in Trissur Pooram

Class Presentations

One night, the students presented a show about the
culture and traditions of Kerala,
India, where they just visited.
The presentations were in drama, dance, and song.
Before the show began, a narrator explained that
the stories would be presented in Katha Kali (Kerala
classical dance), saying:"Katha Kali is one of the
oldest theater forms in the world. It originated in
a region in Southwestern India known today as the
state of Kerala. Katha Kali is a group dance, in which
dancers play various roles traditionally based on
themes from Hindu mythology. The story is told only
with movement and gestures, without words.

"One of the most interesting aspects of Katha Kali is its elaborate makeup. Character makeup is determined by the nature of each character, and is very strictly defined.

"The technique of Katha Kali includes a highly-developed language of gesture, through which the artists relate whole stories."

After she finished the introduction, the group presented the story of Krishna (my favorite story). The next group told the story of King Maveli. The last group explained the celebration of the Trissur Pooram festival. The students who presented Trissur Pooram asked me to help them. Grace made two dummy elephants and I was in the middle. The colorful umbrella demonstration is an unforgettable sight. That's why millions flock from around the world year after year to see the show. At the end of the Pooram celebration, two competing teams display fireworks.

While the students were demonstrating the fireworks for the class, Somali pirates boarded the ship!

Chapter 9

Kris tumbles down into the sea

Pirates Board the Ship

When the electricity went off, everyone first thought that it was part of students' dramatic presentation but I heard gunshots from the deck. Gunshots terrify me! I trumpeted in fright!
I ran wild. I broke all the ankle restraints and ran to the deck, knocking down everything in my path. On deck, I saw four wicked pirates shooting their guns into the air.

People were screaming and running in a panic. The captain of the ship had already been taken hostage.

But I was a surprise. The pirates never expected to see an elephant on the ship. When they saw me, they panicked and began shooting randomly. That frightened me even more. I trumpeted again and ran about the deck, looking for a hiding place! Meanwhile, someone sent an alarm to the engine room and the ship's engines were stopped. We lost all electrical power. The ship was pitch dark. I had no idea where I was running. I broke the guardrail and down I fell, into the cold, salty sea.

Chapter 10

Pirates lock up students and teachers in storage

Jojo and George GetDuct-Taped

The ship was floating on the dark sea, and there was panic and chaos on deck. Students were crying, and the crew had been taken hostage. The teachers were herded to a locked room.

The Somali pirates were prepared. They had flashlights and they were armed and dangerous. The leader of the group told the students that they would not be harmed. The pirates only wanted a ransom. They were to tell their families to send money; instructions for where to send money would follow. Jojo and George resisted the pirates, so they were duct-taped together. They were just looking for me! And I was in the water!

Chapter 11

Kris swims in the sea

Kris's Will to Live

I struggled to keep my trunk up.
Elephants can swim but I had never swum for so
long. This wasn't like swimming across a river. I was
afraid in the dark, and the cold water was chilling my
bones. But I kept on swimming.
I swam and swam just to stay by the drifting boat.
I kept saying to myself, I will not give up; I will pull
through here in this salty ocean.

Chapter 12

Kris rides on a killer whale

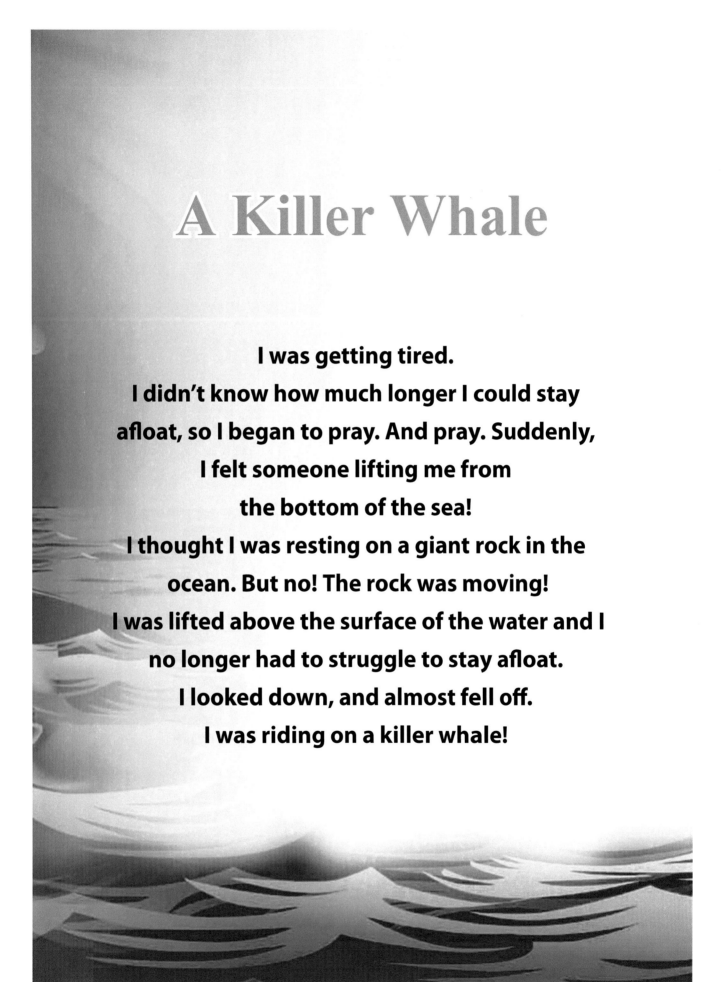

A Killer Whale

I was getting tired.
I didn't know how much longer I could stay
afloat, so I began to pray. And pray. Suddenly,
I felt someone lifting me from
the bottom of the sea!
I thought I was resting on a giant rock in the
ocean. But no! The rock was moving!
I was lifted above the surface of the water and I
no longer had to struggle to stay afloat.
I looked down, and almost fell off.
I was riding on a killer whale!

Chapter 13

The U.S. Navy ship lifts Kris on a net to the ship

Dolphins to Kris's Rescue

Suddenly, all around me, in the sparkling light of the moon, I saw a group of dolphins jumping and playing, and guiding the whale and me. Those little rascals, they are so intelligent that they can communicate even with a huge killer whale.

I was so exhausted that I was hardly aware of the crazy things happening to me as we moved through the water, leaving the ship and the pirates behind.

At some point I felt that I was dreaming. Suddenly the whale stopped. The dolphins circled around us, talking with their shrill voices. I looked up to see an enormous ship looming above us. It was a U.S. Navy ship.

I was dehydrated and exhausted and confused.
Was this all a dream?
The sailors quickly launched a boat to come
alongside the whale and me.

Two brave sailors hopped on the whale's back to
secure a net sling around my middle, and I was
lifted into the air, up to the deck of the ship.
As I reached the railing, I saw the whale and the
dolphins wave their tails in the air, saying their
good-byes, and disappearing into the sea.
Had the U.S. Navy trained these heroes to
save me? I'll never know.
I was exhausted, and now I was scared. Where
was I? How would I find George and Jojo?
I began to trumpet and yell. No one could calm
me down. I was agitated beyond myself. Then
I saw the tranquilizer gun. I became more
agitated, pulling against the ropes that held me.
In all the commotion, someone began shouting
my name. "Kris! Kris! It's Kris the elephant!"
I froze. I looked around. Who could it be, yelling
my name? George and Jojo were on the other
ship. Was this a dream?
Suddenly, I saw him. My friend from Crow Island.
Ravi!

Chapter 14

Ravi hugs Kris

Ravi and Kris

Ravi broke through
the crowd and ran to hug me. "Kris!"
I blew a trumpet blast of delight and wrapped
my trunk around his body,
careful not to hug him too tightly.
Ravi asked Captain Tom to release
the ropes and net.
"Kris is a good tame elephant," Ravi assured
Captain Tom. Seeing that I had calmed down
and showed no signs of struggling, Captain Tom
ordered his men to untie me from the nets.
Ravi was on the ship because he was a part of
a new humanitarian U.S. Navy program that
invited the best and brightest students from
other countries to study in the United States. I
understood his explanation, but he had no idea
how I came to be in the Indian Ocean
close to the African coast.

Captain Tom and Operation Elephant

Ravi asked me what had happened, how I come to be in the ocean, and where Jojo and George were. I pointed to the sea with my trunk. Captain Tom and the crew had heard about the pirates and the ship they had captured. They were on their way to help the captured ship when they found me.

Then Ravi understood. He told the captain that I must have been on that ship; it was the only logical explanation.

A horrifying thought struck the captain. "If that ship has come from India . . . Grace, my daughter. . . Oh no!" he shouted, grabbing Ravi and shaking him in dread. "My daughter is on that ship!"

Chapter 15

Captain Tom called for an emergency meeting of his advisors and the Navy Seals. The meeting concluded with search-and-rescue plans.

Captain Tom meets Ravi

Captain Tom contacted Washington about the mission, explaining the story of the students and of his daughter.

The Mission

The Navy Seals needed my help. They also
needed Ravi's help, since he was
the one I obeyed.
I was excited to be included in the mission to
save the captured students, Jojo, George, and
especially my favorite, Dr. Grace.
Captain Tom received permission to save the
students from the Somali pirates. The mission
was code named "Operation Elephant."
Using my acute sense of smell, I was to direct the
Navy Seals' boat toward the captured vessel in
the darkness of night,

before the moon rose. Radar works well, but my senses work flawlessly and without any sound. I would be their radar.

Team of Navy Seals, Krishna, and Ravi set out on a special mission boat

Navy Seals

The Navy Seals launched their rescue vessel, holding it alongside the ship so I could be lowered in. I was so excited about our mission that I didn't think about being scared or seasick.

Once we approached the area where the captured vessel was drifting, a Navy Seal switched off the lights. We were going in the dark.

Two pirates head to the shore

I'm sure you know that an elephant never forgets, so I had a clear memory of the layout of the cruise ship. I knew where we needed to board if we were to surprise the pirates.

I began sniffing the air, my trunk acting like a radar antenna. Ravi communicated with the Seals. Once he sensed we were near, he patted me and told the Seals, "We're there." The Seals put on their night-vision goggles and watched for the pirated boat. Suddenly, a Navy Seal reported to the captain that two of the pirates had a hostage and were heading toward the shore in a small boat.

"They've got a bargaining chip now," the Seal
reported.
Two Navy Seals slid into the water
with laser guns and other gear.
When they reached the pirate's boat, they
identified the student hostage, bound and
blindfolded on the middle bench. Since the Navy
Seals were using night-vision goggles, they could
clearly see the pirates and the hostage.

The two pirates were armed with machine guns. The Navy Seals ordered the dolphins to distract the pirates, so the dolphins began jumping and splashing in the water at the side of the small boat. When the pirates aimed their guns in the direction of the noise, two of the Navy Seals leapt up to the boat's side and pulled the pirates into the water.

One of the pirates began to scream, "Save me, I don't know how to swim!" I got ready to hop in and save him, but the Navy Seals grabbed him first. The Seals disarmed the pirates, bound them, and threw them into the boat.

They told the hostage as they removed the blindfold, "Do not fear, we are the U.S. Navy."

Dr. Grace

The Navy Seals took the pirates' boat to the rescue boat and helped the hostage to safety. They gave the hostage a warm blanket, then asked her name. "Grace," the hostage answered. They spoke the name into the radio connected to the Navy ship.

Grace in the boat and blindfolded

The captain heard his daughter's voice. "Thank God," he said over the microphone, near tears. "It's your daddy here."

Grace called back at him, "I am okay, Daddy. Thank you for rescuing me!"

The Navy Seals began to question Grace about the situation on the ship regarding the students and teachers, the crew, and the pirates.

Grace was happy to see me as I was standing nearby during the questioning and as soon as she was allowed, she came to hug me. Then she saw Ravi standing on the deck and ran to greet him, too.

Soon the three of us became a team. Ravi could communicate with me, I could communicate with Ravi, and Ravi could communicate with Grace and all the others.

We began to make plans to board the captured cruise ship and disarm all the pirates.

Save the Elephant

Meanwhile, Captain Tom was dealing with Washington politics. Some people did not like the name of the operation. Others said that it was wasting the Navy's resources, and others said that the United States should not fund such operations. As the students' parents and relatives demanded a quick resolution to the hostage crisis,

Strikes and rallies for and against Operation   Elephant

political dithering continued to put
the hostages at terrible risk.
Even animal rights groups began protesting all
over the nation. "Save the elephants!" they shouted.
Some of the newly formed groups collected money
to save me - a rescue project just for me.
Colleges that were involved in the Study at Sea
program released the pictures of the students.
Parents, relatives, friends of those students, and
teachers called their senators and congressmen
to help to save their dear ones, as questions
continued to be debated: Operation Elephant or
Operation Dolphin? Fund the rescue or don't fund
it? The controversy and debates went on and on.
New stories and theories came out
in newspapers and on TV shows.
And still, the pirates held the hostages.

Praying for Children

Families in the United States began to pray for the safety of their children. People were upset by the Washington politicians and their inaction. Some congressmen had the audacity to say that American tax dollars were being wasted for stupid trips to other countries under the pretext of college study. They wanted a congressional hearing of all the college presidents who were involved in this Study at Sea program.

Chapter 20

Some said let us save our children, let us have our priorities straight. Save our citizens.

Operation Grace

A presidential Executive Order was needed. Meanwhile, the operation to save the students and capture the pirates went on without the name. Finally, the president gave a press conference and said, "For goodness sake, let the Navy do the right thing.

Signs all over the TV flash Operation Grace

FLASH NEWS OPERATION GRACE

Chapter 21

Why is Congress politicizing the rescue effort?
It is the life and safety issue of our children and
I am issuing an executive order for Operation
Grace, funded by the Office of the Navy."
One political party threatened to impeach the
president, but people all over the United States
were relieved that the president had finally taken a
courageous stand.
Some critics went on television to voice their
disagreement, accusing the president of raising the
national debt further and further.

Chapter 22

Kris siphons lots of seawater into his trunk and
blows it forcefully at one of the pirates

Elephant Trick

Two Navy Seals donned the captured pirates' clothing and went back into their rescue boat to get onto the disabled ship.

Grace joined us, and we had a plan. Dolphins were brought back to the scene.

There were two pirates with machine guns guarding both ends of the ship. The goal was to capture the pirates without firing a shot or killing anyone.

The dolphins did their trick again as they splashed water vigorously in front of the ship. One guard rushed toward the noise and aimed his machine gun at the dolphins in the dark, but dolphins were so quick he could not get a clear shot, or see anything in the water.

As he hung over the side railing, I siphoned lots
of seawater into my trunk and blew it forcefully at
him. He came crashing down into the water, losing
his machine gun to the bottom of the sea.
I picked him out of the water and put him into our
boat. Grace and Ravi bound him with a rope.
Meanwhile, the Navy Seals were
climbing onto the ship.

As they climbed up, the second pirate recognized the caps of their buddies and didn't shoot, thinking that help had arrived from shore.

The Navy Seals were unaware that they were being watched by armed pirate son the ship. But I took position in the boat, siphoned more water into my trunk, and got ready for action.

The dolphins made another big splash to divert the lone pirate's attention and he leaned over to look again at the noisy area.

I let go a huge spray of water and he tumbled down into the deep sea.

I immediately picked him up with my trunk and tossed him into the boat, and Grace and Ravi did their job of tying him down. Suddenly, I felt that capturing these Somali pirates was a piece of cake.

Sighs of Relief

Navy Seals went around the ship and announced that they were members of the U.S. Navy and that the pirates were all in their custody. First, Jojo and George were released from their restraints, and they in turn directed the Navy Seals to the holding cells where the students and teachers were being held.

The ship's crew was also released from their holding cells. They were all relieved.

Captain Tom sent the good news to the White House: "Mission accomplished without a shot fired."

Since the ship had suffered extensive damage, it needed to be towed and repaired. The U.S. Navy ship came to transfer all the students, teachers, and the crew from the disabled cruise ship. The students and teachers were extremely glad to see Dr. Grace safe and unharmed.

Chapter 23

After I was once again lifted by a crane back onto the Navy ship, Jojo and George greeted me with a huge hug. They could not believe that I was able to save everyone in the ship, with the cooperation of dolphins, a killer whale, and the U.S. Navy.

But in my mind, I said that once again Ravi
had saved my life and was instrumental to this
Operation Elephant. . . sorry, Operation Dolphin, or
rather, Operation Grace.

The Navy ship was returning to her home port in San Diego, so Grace told Captain Tom that the San Diego Zoo would be an ideal place for me to live, as its climate was warmer, like that of Kochi. Unfortunately, in Washington, another hurdle erupted regarding our arrival-Jojo, George, and me.

Mission Accomplished

It seems I required a medical checkup before I
could enter the United States.

Dr. Grace wanted to send me to the San Diego Wild
Animal Park or San Diego Zoo for a checkup and
rehabilitation after my ordeal at sea, but first we
had to get permission for me to enter the country.
The disabled ship was to be repaired but, luckily,
the Navy ship was scheduled to be in San Diego.
Permission was requested for both Jojo and George
to be given visas to enter the United States as my
handlers (the other visas had been for Saint-Dennis
Island and were not good in the United States).
I had to go through the quarantine process on
the ship itself, but we were not sure whether
Immigration and Customs would ever allow me to
set foot in San Diego, or send me back to India.

Chapter 24

My only comfort during the waiting period was Grace and Ravi. Their care and dedication made my waiting and quarantine time easier. Meanwhile, on land, the parents were delighted to hear that their children were safe. They were anxious to see them and embrace them. The teachers and the Study at Sea crew, free from the pirates' cruel treatment, couldn't wait to reach home.

Navy's medical team checks both Jojo and George

The news, Mission Accomplished, was in all the media. As usual, the politics regarding us was controversial. Some said that they didn't want any illegal aliens coming into the country (meaning Jojo and George). Those people had to go back to their country and get visas, they declared. They were also against me coming to America, because they said it would be a tremendous burden on the country to feed an elephant.

Fortunately, the American children wanted to see me. They wrote to their congressmen, senators, and to the president, asking them to allow me to come into the United States. At many schools, the children collected their lunch money and sent it to the U.S. Treasury to fund my upkeep.

College and university students picketed and organized demonstrations against the political wrangling regarding Jojo, George, and me. I also had lots of support from the Hollywood community, late night shows, and even the animal rights groups.

Young Lovers

Captain Tom sent requests to Washington to grant immediate emergency visas for Jojo and George, and, of course, for me, too. The Homeland Security Office carefully debated and then processed the captain's request.

I was happy to be under the care of Dr. Grace. Jojo and George were new to the American lifestyle and were looking forward to enjoying their new experiences. Ravi would continue his studies at the local university as an exchange student.

I heard Ravi say to Dr. Grace that he would like to attend a university close to the zoo where I would be cared for. Dr. Grace seemed to be willing to help. It seemed to me that they liked each other. I hoped they would fall in love.

Chapter 25

Grace and Ravi, young lovers

Kris, Welcome to America

A big reception was planned for the rescue team at the San Diego Harbor terminal. Students, family members, various university representatives, thousands of San Diegans, and some political leaders were ready at the pier to receive the Study at Sea students and me. Many were curious to see the elephant who had knocked down the pirates with water from its trunk.

Children from all over the world had read in newspapers about the fascinating story of my involvement in capturing the Somali pirates. Many children urged their parents to take them to San Diego to see me. I love children and they love me, too. When the Navy ship arrived, we were still unsure as to whether Jojo and George and I would be allowed to live in the United States.

Chapter 26

Parade of students, teachers, crews, Navy
Seals, Captain Tom, Jojo, George, Ravi,
Grace, and Me (Kris, the elephant)

People on shore waited and waited for final word.
Cell phones were ringing, text messages were
flying, and cell photo tweets were
jamming the system.

But still there were no answers, so Jojo, George, and
I stayed on the ship. The students from Semester at
Sea, teachers, and the crew cleared both

Kris dreams about the Golden Emblem on
his back

the Immigration and Customs, but they refused to leave without us. They saved our lives by sticking around and demanding answers.

Finally, the people's demand won. Their determination to do the right thing came through. When the U.S. Immigration cleared visas for Jojo and George, a ceremonial visa was stamped especially for me to keep in the file. The pirates were sent to immigration holding cells, where they were to wait for trail. They seemed to be pleading with the authorities not to send them to Guantanamo.

When I came out from the immigration and customs office, both Grace and Ravi were riding on me. Dr. Grace had become my personal doctor as well as a good friend. Jojo and George walked side by side with me on the pier.

I could hear the cheers and shouts of joy from the people who were waiting. "Look, look, here comes the elephant!"

I looked around the city and the harbor. It reminded me of Kochi Harbor with the ships, the bay, and the beautiful tall buildings; instead of coconut trees, I saw the graceful, swaying palm trees.

Thunderous applause greeting Captain Tom, who was accompanied by Navy Seals and the crew as he stepped off the ship.

One child from the audience wanted to give me a banana. Captain Tom picked up the child and carried her over to me. I gently stretched my trunk and bent down to receive the banana. The child said to me, "Welcome to the USA."

The End

Printed in the United States
By Bookmasters